Look what I can do

by Jose Aruego

Aladdin Books
Macmillan Publishing Company • New York

for Kit and Bud

Copyright © 1971 by Jose Aruego

Aladdin Books
Macmillan Publishing Company
866 Third Avenue, New York, NY 10022
Collier Macmillan Canada, Inc.

First Aladdin Books edition 1988

Printed in the United States of America

10   9   8   7   6   5   4   3   2

Library of Congress Cataloging-in-Publication Data

Aruego, Jose.
    Look what I can do / by Jose Aruego. — 1st Aladdin
Books ed.
    p.   cm.
    Summary: Two carabaos discover that being a copycat
can lead to trouble.
    ISBN 0-689-71205-7 (pbk.)
    [1. Water buffalo — Fiction. 2. Behavior — Fiction.]
I. Title.
PZ7.A7475Lo   1988
[E] — dc19   87-21743
                                       CIP
                                       AC

A carabao who herds with a fence jumper becomes a fence jumper too.

OLD PHILIPPINE PROVERB

Look what I can do!

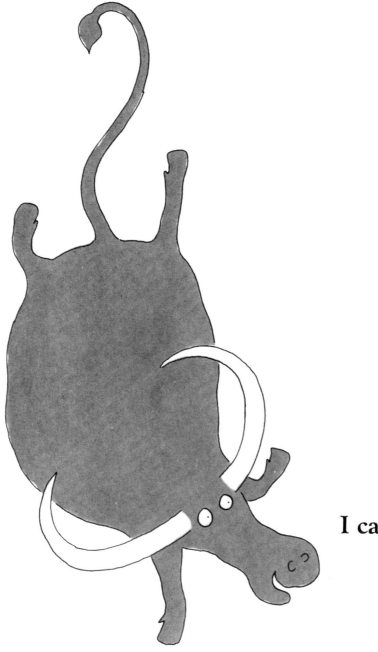

I can do it too!

Look what I can do!